I Can Fix It!

I Can Fix It!

Robert Munsch

Illustrations by
Michael Martchenko

Scholastic Canada Ltd.
Toronto New York London Auckland Sydney
Mexico City New Delhi Hong Kong Buenos Aires

Scholastic Canada Ltd.
604 King Street West, Toronto, Ontario M5V 1E1, Canada

Scholastic Inc.
557 Broadway, New York, NY 10012, USA

Scholastic Australia Pty Limited
PO Box 579, Gosford, NSW 2250, Australia

Scholastic New Zealand Limited
Private Bag 94407, Botany, Manukau 2163, New Zealand

Scholastic Children's Books
Euston House, 24 Eversholt Street, London NW1 1DB, UK

www.scholastic.ca

The art for this book was painted in watercolour on Crescent illustration board.
The type is set in 19 point Excelsior LT.

Library and Archives Canada Cataloguing in Publication

Title: I can fix it! / Robert Munsch ; illustrated by Michael Martchenko.
Names: Munsch, Robert N., 1945- author. | Martchenko, Michael, illustrator.
Description: Published simultaneously in hardcover by North Winds Press.
Identifiers: Canadiana 20210238984 | ISBN 9781443192125 (softcover)
Classification: LCC PS8576.U575 I23 2021b | DDC jC813/.54—dc23

Title page drawing by Taylor Perry.

6 5 4 3 2 1   Printed in Canada 119   21 22 23 24 25

*For Taylor Perry,
Kelowna, British Columbia
— R.M.*

When Taylor was a baby, her mother gave her a blanket, the very best blanket in the world. And Taylor took hold of that blanket and wouldn't let go.

3

When she was
one, she lay on it.

When she was two,
she sucked on the
corner and dragged it
around the house.

When she was three,
she sucked on the
corner and dragged it
around outside.

4

When she was four, she sucked on the corner and took it on her tricycle.

When she was five, she sucked on the corner, took it to kindergarten, and kept it in her cubby.

5

When she was six, she still carried that blanket everywhere.

Until the day her big brother, Jordan, stole it.

Actually, he borrowed it. He had spilled chocolate ice cream on the kitchen floor and used the blanket to clean it up.

When he was done, he washed
out the blanket in the kitchen sink,
but it still had a brown spot on it.

So he put lemon juice on the spot
and it turned yellow.

9

Then he put window cleaner on the spot and it turned green.

Then he soaked the whole blanket in dishwasher detergent and the spot turned dark purple and the blanket shrank and got all wrinkled and scratchy.

Jordan hid the blanket under the couch cushions and hoped that Taylor would not find it.

But Taylor found it anyway, and she did not like the changes to her blanket. She started to yell and scream:

AAAHHHHHHHHHHHHH!

AAAHHHHHHHHHHHHH!

AAAHHHHHHHHHHHHHH!

Jordan came running and said, "Taylor, be quiet! It's just a blanket!"

Taylor screamed louder:

AAAHHHHHHHHHHHH!

AAAHHHHHHHHHHHHH!

YOU KILLED MY BLANKET!

Jordan yelled, "TAYLOR!
YOU ARE TOO BIG FOR A
BABY BLANKET ANYWAY!"
Taylor yelled the loudest
yell possible:

AAAHHHHHHHHHHHH!
YOU KILLED MY BLANKET!
YOU ARE A TERRIBLE BROTHER!

She ran into Jordan's room and started throwing his clothes and books and teenager stuff all over the place.

Taylor's mother came in and yelled:

TAYLOR, STOP IT! STOP IT! STOP IT RIGHT NOW!

Taylor stood in the middle of the mess and said, "Jordan wrecked my blanket! It's all messed up!"

Her mom gave her a hug and said, "I think I can fix it."

She took Taylor to the attic and opened up an old box.

"Look, Taylor," she said. "This is the blanket your grandma gave me when I was a baby.

"When I was one,
I lay on it.

"When I was two,
I dragged it around the house.

"When I was three,
I dragged it around outside.

"When I was four,
I took it on my tricycle.

"When I was six, I used it to wrap up my favourite doll.

"When I was five, I took it to kindergarten and kept it in my cubby."

"And I have kept it ever since."

23

"It's a very nice blanket," said Taylor.

"Yes, it is a nice blanket," said her mom. "And now it's yours!"

Taylor smiled and gave her mom an enormous hug.

Taylor took her new blanket downstairs and wrapped it around her doll.

And then she went to fix up her brother's room.